STATUE of LIBERTY and ELLIS ISLAND Coloring Book

A. G. Smith

Dover Publications, Inc.
Mineola, New York

Bibliographical Note

BOOST Statue of Liberty and Ellis Island Coloring Book, first published by Dover Publications, Inc., in 2013, is a revised edition of *Statue of Liberty and Ellis Island Coloring Book*, originally published by Dover in 1985.

International Standard Book Number
ISBN-13: 978-0-486-49419-7
ISBN-10: 0-486-49419-5

Manufactured in the United States by Courier Corporation
49419501   2013
www.doverpublications.com

Introduction

Since 1886 the *Statue of Liberty* (actually titled *Liberty Enlightening the World*) has stood in New York Harbor, a gift from France commemorating Franco-American friendship. But over the years the statue has gained in meaning. Now it also symbolizes the millions of immigrants who came to this country and the United States itself.

The idea of giving a colossal statue to the United States was first planted in the mind of Frédéric-Auguste Bartholdi at a dinner party in 1865, when the recent assassination of Abraham Lincoln had evoked a tremendous outpouring of sympathy from the French. Bartholdi, then 31, was already noted as a sculptor. But it was not until 1871 that conditions were right to go ahead with the project. In the meantime, Bartholdi had executed several models for a Suez lighthouse (never built), showing elements that were incorporated into the *Statue of Liberty*. With France recovering from the Franco-Prussian War and the bloodbath of the Paris Commune, Bartholdi went to the United States to enlist American support for the project. In New York he decided that Bedloe's (now Liberty) Island would be the ideal site for the statue.

It took years of politicking, but eventually the French raised sufficient funds to have the statue built. The original target date had been 1876—in time for the centennial celebration of American independence. That proved impossible. The statue was laboriously produced piecemeal in a Parisian workshop between 1876 and 1881. Then the work was assembled outside, on the ingenious framework designed by Gustave Eiffel, rising over the rooftops to the astonishment of the city. The statue was formally presented to the American ambassador, then was disassembled and shipped to New York, arriving in May 1885. The French had fulfilled their part of the plan. The Americans were slow to complete their end: construction of the pedestal on which the statue was to stand. Unfortunately, the project had not generated much enthusiasm in this country. The efforts of Joseph Pulitzer, through his newspaper *The World*, finally raised the money needed. The pedestal, designed by Richard Morris Hunt, one of America's leading architects, was constructed on old Fort Wood; the statue was assembled and was unveiled on October 28, 1886.

Thereafter the statue was the first great American landmark seen by immigrants as they entered New York harbor on steamer after steamer. Immigration had been the lifeblood of America from the earliest years, but its nature had changed. Starting in the 1840s, when potato rot had destroyed the Irish potato crops, the volume of immigration had increased dramatically. Many of the newcomers lacked the skills that earlier immigrants had possessed. In the 1870s there was a great influx from southern Europe. At the end of the century, Jews fleeing the pogroms of Eastern Europe swelled the numbers of people trying to establish a new life in the United States.

For years immigration into this country by way of New York had been under the supervision of the city. Arriving immigrants were processed at Castle Garden, which had served first as a fort (Castle Clinton), then as a center of entertainment. But when the city bureaucracy was swamped by the rising number of immigrants, the federal government assumed the load. Castle Clinton was closed (it later reopened as an aquarium and is now restored to its original apearance) and in 1892 new facilities were inaugurated on Ellis Island.

Immigration reached a peak in 1907, when 1,285,239 people passed through the station. To those who had already endured much, this was perhaps the most terrifying part of the long journey, for any immigrant failing to pass inspection would be detained and sent back to Europe. Having passed inspection, newcomers were ferried across the bay to New York City, where they were faced with the formidable task of establishing themselves in an environment unlike any they had ever encountered. Many immigrants simply passed through New York, moving on to the West, spurred by the vision of owning rich farmland, but a good number settled in the city, the largest concentration being on the Lower East Side, reputedly the most densely populated area in the world at the turn of the century.

Conditions on the Lower East Side were hard: Families were jammed into dilapidated tenements, work was grinding and low-paying. Yet the Lower East Side possessed a vitality that has become legendary.

While the immigrants' lives involved struggle and sacrifice, many of the new Americans prospered and made contributions that have altered and enriched American society.

NOTE: Most of the illustrations in this book are based on historical paintings, wood engravings that appeared in contemporary newspapers and magazines, and photographs taken from various sources.

The *Statue of Liberty* is recognized as a symbol of the United States. It was a gift to America from France.

 RI.1.2 Identify the main topic and retell key details of a text. Also **RI.1.6, RI.1.7, RF.1.4, L.1.6; RI.2.6, RI.2.7, RF.2.4, L.2.6.**

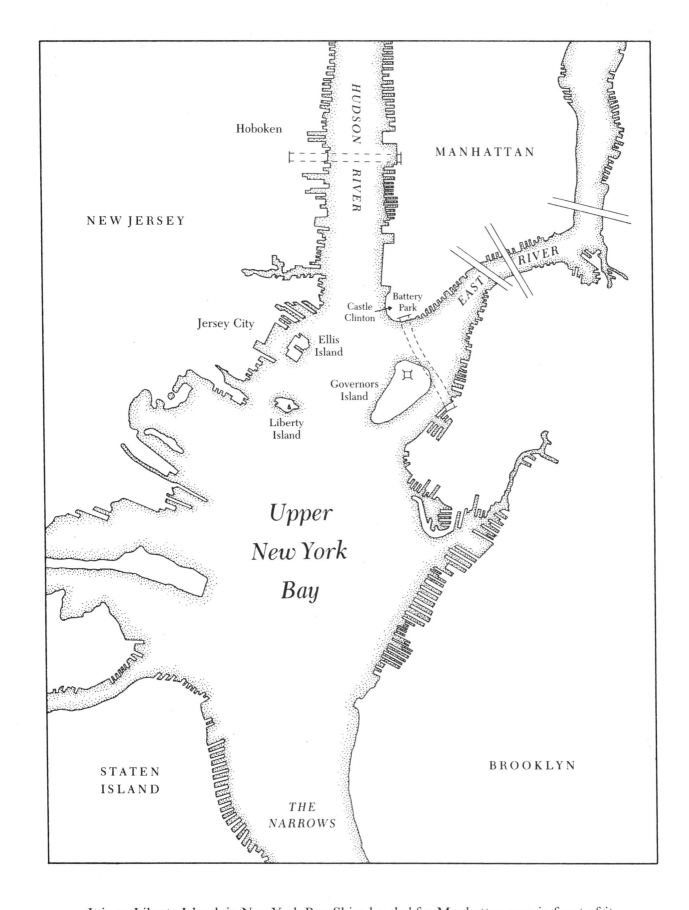

It is on Liberty Island, in New York Bay. Ships headed for Manhattan pass in front of it.

CCSS **RI.1.7** Use the illustrations and details in a text to describe its key ideas. Also **RI.1.1, RI.1.4, SL.1.2; RI.2.1, RI.2.4, RI.2.7, SL.2.2.**

Frédéric Auguste Bartholdi was the sculptor who designed it. He wanted to give it to America.

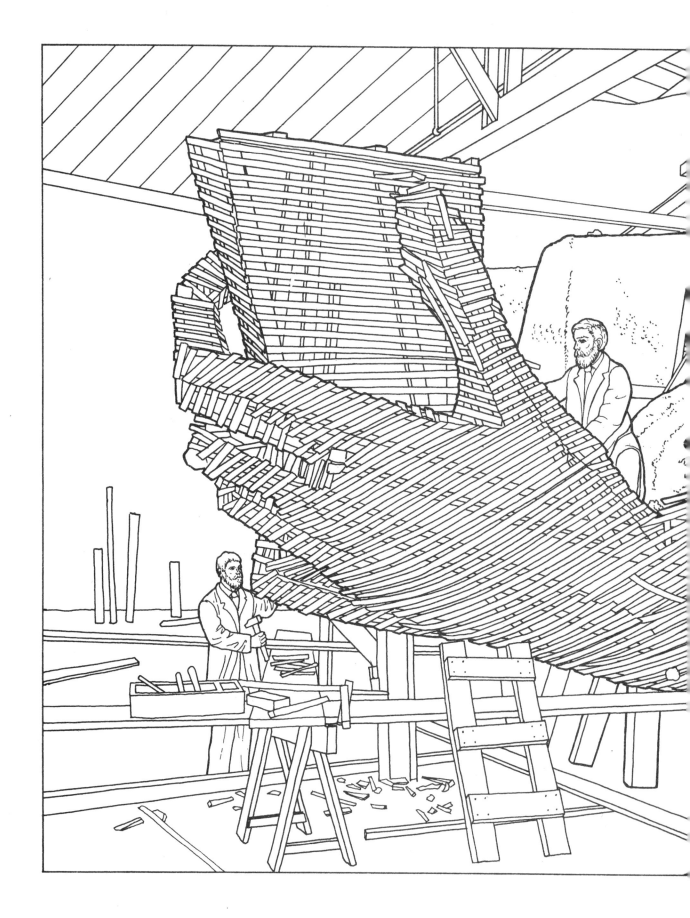

 RI.1.6 Distinguish between information provided by pictures or other illustrations and information provided by the words in a text. Also **RI.1.1, RI.1.7, SL.1.2, SL.1.4; RI.2.1, RI.2.6, RI.2.7, SL.2.2.**

The French raised money to build the statue. It was made out of wood and plaster. It was covered in copper.

In 1876 the hand with the torch was sent to the United States. First, it was shown in Philadelphia. Then it moved to New York. Five years later, it went back to France.

 RI.1.2 Identify the main topic and retell key details of a text. Also **RI.1.7, RI.1.10, L.1.6; RI.2.7, RI.2.10, L.2.6.**

The framework of the statue was designed by Alexandre-Gustave Eiffel. He also designed the Eiffel Tower. It was made in Paris.

 RI.1.1 Ask and answer questions about key details in a text. Also **RI.1.4, RF.1.4, L.1.4; RI.2.1, RI.2.4, RF.2.4, L.2.4.**

On July 4, 1884 it was given to the American ambassador to France. Then it was taken apart. It was sent to New York in separate pieces.

The pedestal was built, and assembly began. The statue made workmen look very small.

 RI.1.4 Ask and answer questions to help determine or clarify the meaning of words and phrases in a text. Also **RI.1.7, RF.1.4.a, SL.1.2; RI.2.4, RF.2.4.a, SL.2.2.**

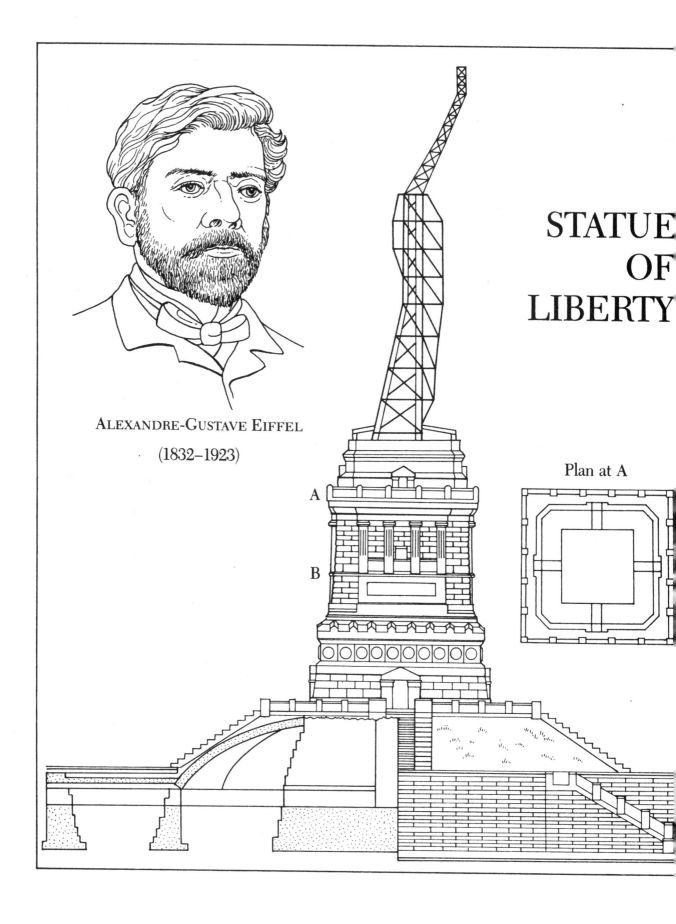

ALEXANDRE-GUSTAVE EIFFEL

(1832–1923)

STATUE
OF
LIBERTY

Plan at A

A

B

 RI.1.7 Use the illustrations and details in a text to describe its key ideas. Also **RI.1.1, RI.1.3, RI.1.4, SL.1.1.c; RI.2.1, RI.2.4, RI.2.7, SL.2.1.c, L.2.4.d.**

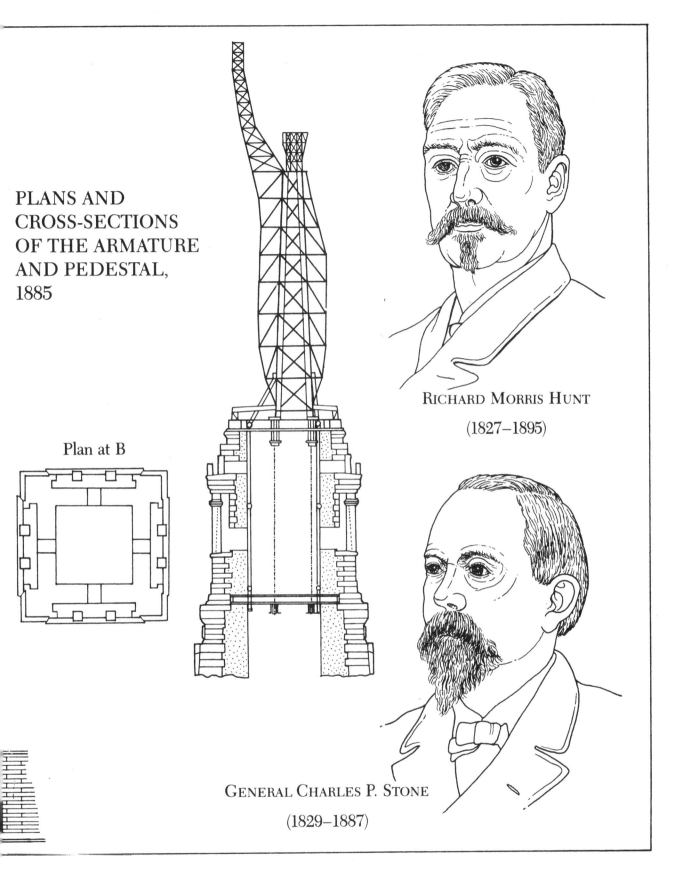

PLANS AND
CROSS-SECTIONS
OF THE ARMATURE
AND PEDESTAL,
1885

Plan at B

Richard Morris Hunt

(1827–1895)

General Charles P. Stone

(1829–1887)

The pedestal was designed by Richard Morris Hunt. He was one of the most important architects at that time.

The face of the *Statue of Liberty* is 10 feet wide. Her face was modeled after the designer's mother.

 RI.1.6 Distinguish between information provided by pictures or other illustrations and information provided by the words in a text. Also **RI.1.1, RI.1.3, L.1.6; RI.2.1, RI.2.6, L.2.6.**

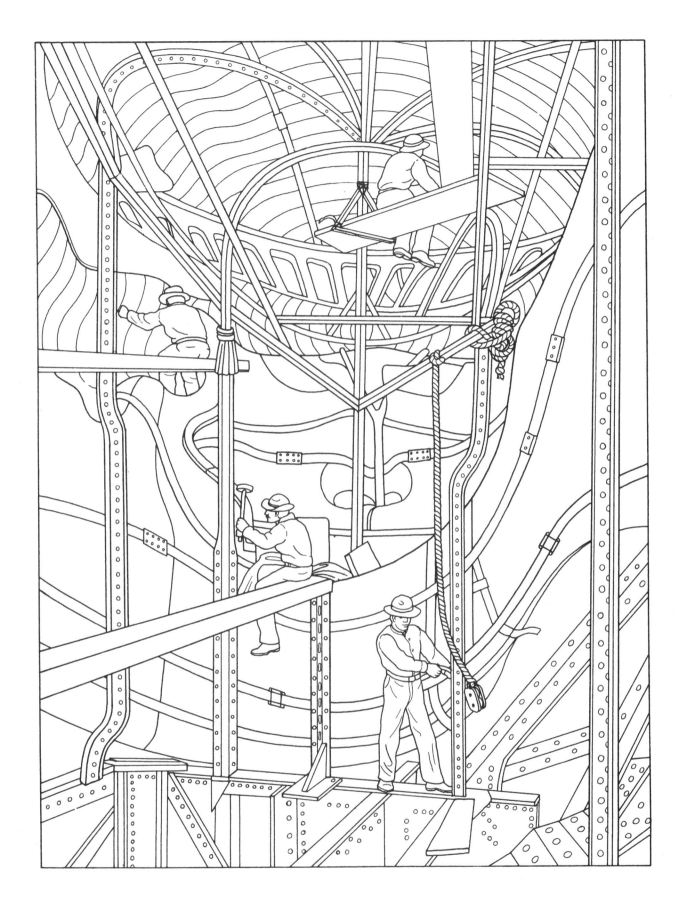

Workers worked inside of the statue to finish the face.

 RI.1.7 Use the illustrations and details in a text to describe its key ideas. Also **RI.1.1, RF.1.4, SL.1.1; RI.2.1, RF.2.4, SL.2.1.**

The head was completed. The seven rays symbolize the seven continents and seven seas on Earth.

 RI.1.6 Distinguish between information provided by pictures or other illustrations and information provided by the words in a text. Also **RI.1.4, SL.1.2, L.1.6; RI.2.4, RI.2.6, SL.2.2, L.2.6.**

On October 28, 1886, the *Statue of Liberty* was unveiled before a huge crowd. President Grover Cleveland was there.

The statue was finished at a time when a lot of immigrants were coming to America.

 RI.1.4 Ask and answer questions to help determine or clarify the meaning of words and phrases in a text. Also **RI.1.1, RF.1.4.a, SL.1.1.c, L.1.4.a; RI.2.4, RF.2.4.a, SL.2.1.c, L.2.4.a.**

The trip to America on ships was long and hard. This picture is based on a real photograph.

 RI.1.7 Use the illustrations and details in a text to describe its key ideas. Also **RI.1.3, RF.1.3, SL.1.1, L.1.4.b; RI.2.7, RF.2.3, SL.2.1, L.2.4.c.**

Many Europeans travelled in the lower part of the ship. People felt the most movement in the lower part of the ship. Many people got sick. This picture is based on a real photograph too.

 RI.1.6 Distinguish between information provided by pictures or other illustrations and information provided by the words in a text. Also **RI.1.4, RI.1.10, SL.1.2, SL.1.4; RI.2.4, RI.2.6, SL.2.2.**

The New Colossus

Not like the brazen giant of Greek fame,
With conquering limbs astride from land to land;
Here at our sea-washed, sunset-gates shall stand
A mighty woman with a torch, whose flame
Is the imprisoned lightning, and her name
Mother of Exiles. From her beacon-hand
Glows world-wide welcome; her mild eyes command
The air-bridged harbor that twin-cities frame.

"Keep, ancient lands, your storied pomp!" cries she
With silent lips. "Give me your tired, your poor,
Your huddled masses yearning to breathe free,
The wretched refuse of your teeming shore.
Send these, the homeless, tempest-tost to me,
I lift my lamp beside the golden door!"

In 1903 a poem was put on the base of the statue. The poem is called "The New Colossus."

RI.1.3 Describe the connection between two individuals, events, ideas, or pieces of information in a text. Also **RI.1.4, RI.1.6, RF.1.3, L.1.6; RI.2.4, RI.2.6, RF.2.3, L.2.6.**

Here is the *Statue of Liberty.* New Jersey is in the background.

By World War I, many immigrants had come to this country. The statue had become a symbol of the United States.

RI.1.3 Describe the connection between two individuals, events, ideas, or pieces of information in a text. Also **RI.1.4, RF.1.3.g, RF.1.4, SL.1.1.c; RI.2.3, RI.2.4, RF.2.3.f, RF.2.4, SL.2.1.c.**

Immigrants used to enter the United States through Castle Garden. It was a round building with a flag. Then they entered through Ellis Island until it closed in 1954.

Some immigration buildings burned down. In 1898 a new building opened. It is still there today. The island is now a national monument.

1903 was the year with the most immigrants. Ellis Island let in thousands of people a day.

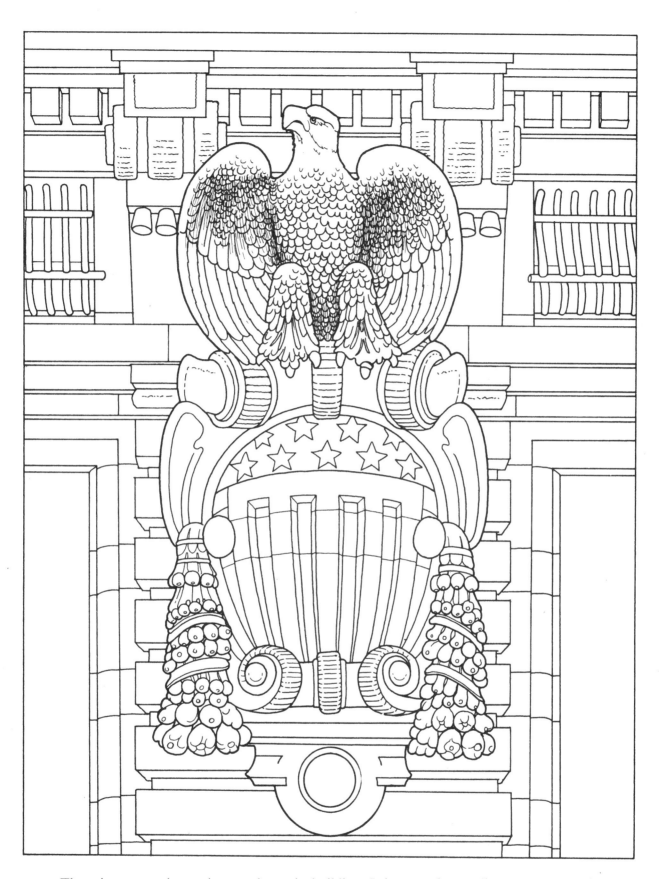

There is a stone decoration on the main building. It is an eagle standing over a coat of arms. The coat of arms has the stars and stripes.

 RI.1.7 Use the illustrations and details in a text to describe its key ideas. Also **RI.1.4, RI.1.6, SL.1.4, L.1.5; RI.2.4, RI.2.6, RI.2.7, L.2.5.**

This picture of immigrants is based on a real photograph. They are carrying their only belongings with them.

 RI.1.1 Ask and answer questions about key details in a text. Also **RI.1.7, RF.1.4, RF.1.3.f, L.1.4.b; RI.2.1, RI.2.7, RF.2.4, RF.2.3.d, L.2.4.c.**

All newcomers had to pass medical examinations. If they failed, they were sent back to Europe.

 RI.1.3 Describe the connection between two individuals, events, ideas, or pieces of information in a text. Also **RI.1.4, RI.1.7, SL.1.2, SL.1.4; RI.2.3, RI.2.4, RI.2.7, SL.2.2.**

29

Many people came to America wearing traditional clothes.

 RI.1.7 Use the illustrations and details in a text to describe its key ideas. Also **RI.1.1,
RF.1.3.f, SL.1.4, L.1.4.b; RI.2.1, RI.2.7, RF.2.3.d, SL.2.2, L.2.4.c.**

Here you can see a family on Ellis Island.

After going through inspection on Ellis Island, immigrants wait for the ferry. It will take them to Manhattan.

 RI.1.3 Describe the connection between two individuals, events, ideas, or pieces of information in a text. Also **RI.1.4, RF.1.4, SL.1.2; RI.2.3, RI.2.4, RF.2.4, SL.2.2.**

Some lucky immigrants had friends or relatives who were already in the city. This man searches for an address in New York.

Many immigrants supported themselves by making clothing. This picture is based on a real photograph.

 RI.1.1 Ask and answer questions about key details in a text. Also **RI.1.7, RF.1.3.f, SL.1.1; RI.2.1, RI.2.7, RF.2.3.d, SL.2.1.**

Other women worked in sweatshops. This work was hard and dangerous. The pay was very low. Many people died or got hurt in fires.

 RI.1.4 Ask and answer questions to help determine or clarify the meaning of words and phrases in a text. Also **RI.1.3, SL.1.4, L.1.4; RI.2.3, RI.2.4, L.2.4.d.**

Pushcarts crowded the streets. Many families made a living selling spices and food from them. These areas became great outdoor markets.

 RI.1.6 Distinguish between information provided by pictures or other illustrations and information provided by the words in a text. Also **RI.1.4, RF.1.3.f, SL.1.1.c, L.1.4.a; RI.2.4, RI.2.6, RF.2.3.d, SL.2.1.c, L.2.4.d.**

Two women chat on the front steps. Many immigrants kept the clothing of their native lands.

Immigrant children learned to play American sports. This picture is based on a real photograph.

 RI.1.6 Distinguish between information provided by pictures or other illustrations and information provided by the words in a text. Also **RI.1.2, RF.1.4, L.1.4.b; RI.2.6, RF.2.4, L.2.4.c.**

Not all immigrants stayed in New York City. This coal miner went to Pennsylvania to find a job.

 RI.1.7 Use the illustrations and details in a text to describe its key ideas. Also **RI.1.1, RI.1.3, L.1.6; RI.2.1, RI.2.3, RI.2.7, L.2.6.**

RI.1.6 Distinguish between information provided by pictures or other illustrations and information provided by the words in a text. Also **RI.1.4, RI.1.7, SL.1.2, SL.1.4, L.1.4; RI.2.4, RI.2.6, RI.2.7, SL.2.2, L.2.4.d.**

Railroad companies and governments wanted immigrants to settle in the west. They offered people in Europe free land. Many people immigrated to the northern Midwest.

Famous Immigrants: Irving Berlin was a popular composer. 2. Knute Rockne was a Football Coach at the University of Notre Dame. 3. Felix Frankfurter was an adviser to President Franklin D. Roosevelt. He later became a Supreme Court justice. 4. Emma Goldman was a social activist. She was deported for her radical views.

CCSS **RI.1.4** Ask and answer questions to help determine or clarify the meaning of words and phrases in a text. Also **RI.1.2, RF.1.4.a, SL.1.1.c; RI.2.2, RI.2.4, RF.2.4., SL.2.1.c.**

5. Paul Muni was a famous actor. 6. Ben Shahn was a socially conscious painter. 7. Father Edward Flanagan was a Roman Catholic priest and social worker. 8. Elia Kazan was a film and play director. He directed many movies based on his novel about immigration.

 RI.1.2 Identify the main topic and retell key details of a text. Also **RI.1.4, RI.1.10, SL.1.1, SL.1.1.c; RI.2.2, RI.2.4, RI.2.10, SL.2.1, SL.2.1.c.**